Ruth Bader Ginsburg's Dream for Justice : A Bedtime Story

By Cody Dragon

ISBN: 9798370853333

DEDICATION

I dedicate this book to my son Ezra Dragon - you've changed my life in ways you'll never know. Always remember to do what is right, especially when it's tough.

Once upon a time, in a time not so far away

There lived a lady named Ruth Bader Ginsburg, they say.

Ruth Bader Ginsburg's Dream for Justice - A Bedtime Story

She was a judge, and a very smart one too,

And she always worked hard to do what was true.

Ruth loved the law and she
loved to learn,

She spent her days reading
and studying, in turn.

She worked hard and she
served with great pride,

She made sure that justice
was always on her side.

So Ruth decided to fight with her all of her might

and worked hard to make sure that women had equal rights

One day, Ruth was appointed
to the highest court,

She was thrilled, and so were
her friends who showed
her support.

Ruth Bader Ginsburg was a hero to all,

She showed us that with hard work, we can stand tall.

So if you're feeling tired and you need some rest,

Just remember Ruth Bader Ginsburg, and do your very best.

Dream big and work hard, and
you too can shine like Ruth

Goodnight and sweet dreams,
little one it's bedtime
for you!

THE END

THE END

www.ingramcontent.com/pod-product-compliance
Lightning Source LLC
LaVergne TN
LVHW071227160826
845679LV00003B/927

9798370853333